Cedar Waxwings

Red Fox

White-tailed Deer

Hairy Woodpecker

Porcupine

Once Upon a Winter Day

Liza Woodruff

MARGARET FERGUSON BOOKS
HOLIDAY HOUSE · NEW YORK

For my friend, Sue Smith, and for others like her
who love and care for our beautiful planet.

The publisher wishes to thank Alison Thomas and Alyssa Bennett from
Vermont Fish and Wildlife, Dan Lambert from Center for Northern Woodlands Education,
and Amy Kuenzi at Montana Tech for their expert review of the text.

Margaret Ferguson Books
Copyright © 2020 by Liza Woodruff
All rights reserved
HOLIDAY HOUSE is registered in the U.S. Patent and Trademark Office.
Printed and bound in June 2020 at Tien Wah Press, Johor Bahru, Johor, Malaysia.
The artwork was created with mixed media: watercolor, pen and ink, colored pencil, and Photoshop.
www.holidayhouse.com
First Edition
1 3 5 7 9 10 8 6 4 2
Library of Congress Cataloging-in-Publication Data

Names: Woodruff, Liza, author.
Title: Once upon a winter day / Liza Woodruff.
Description: First edition. | New York : Holiday House, [2020]
"Margaret Ferguson Books." | Audience: Ages 4–8. | Audience: Grades K–1.
Summary: "Milo's mother is too busy to read him a story so she sends him
outside to play in the snow where he discovers a story of his own"
–Provided by publisher. | Identifiers: LCCN 2019039866
ISBN 9780823440993 (hardcover)
Subjects: CYAC: Nature–Fiction. | Winter–Fiction. | Storytelling–Fiction.
Classification: LCC PZ7.W8615 Onc 2020 | DDC [E]—dc23
LC record available at https://lccn.loc.gov/2019039866

Milo was looking for a story but his mother was busy.
"Why don't you go play in the snow?" she asked.

Milo bundled up and plodded outside.
He didn't want to play in the snow; he wanted a story.

He stomped a path from the house to the birdfeeder.
Beneath the feeder, tiny footprints sprinkled the ground.
"A mouse was here," said Milo.

Did the mouse have a story to tell?

Milo followed the tracks to the winterberry bush.
All the red berries had disappeared.

As he brushed the branches, snow fell away revealing a single feather.

What had happened here?

A cold wind crept beneath Milo's scarf.
The trail led into the shelter of the forest.

Beneath the hemlock trees, branches littered the ground.

Why had they fallen like autumn leaves?

Milo wove through the trees, trailing the little prints.
Loose clods of dirt scattered at his feet.

Who had dug beneath the snow?

Had they been looking for acorns?

Milo's breath rose in clouds as he hurried onward.
He followed the tracks out of the trees until
he came to the creek.

A smooth rut slid down the bank.

Who had been gliding in the snow?

Milo zigged and zagged away from
the creek and across the field.
He followed the footprints until suddenly
they stopped.

Something had brushed the tiny tracks away.

KEEARRR!

Had the bird calling in the distance swooped
to the snow?

MILO! DINNER TIME!

"Darn!" said Milo.
Was it really time to go inside?

He headed home, walking beside the tiny footprints until they disappeared down a hole.

Maybe the mouse had gone home too.

Inside, the smell of soup made Milo's stomach grumble.

"Do you want me to read you some stories after dinner?" his mother asked.
Milo shook his head as he laid out what he had found.
"This time," he said, "I have stories for you."

Northern
Cardinal

River Otters

Deer
Mouse

Red-tailed Hawks